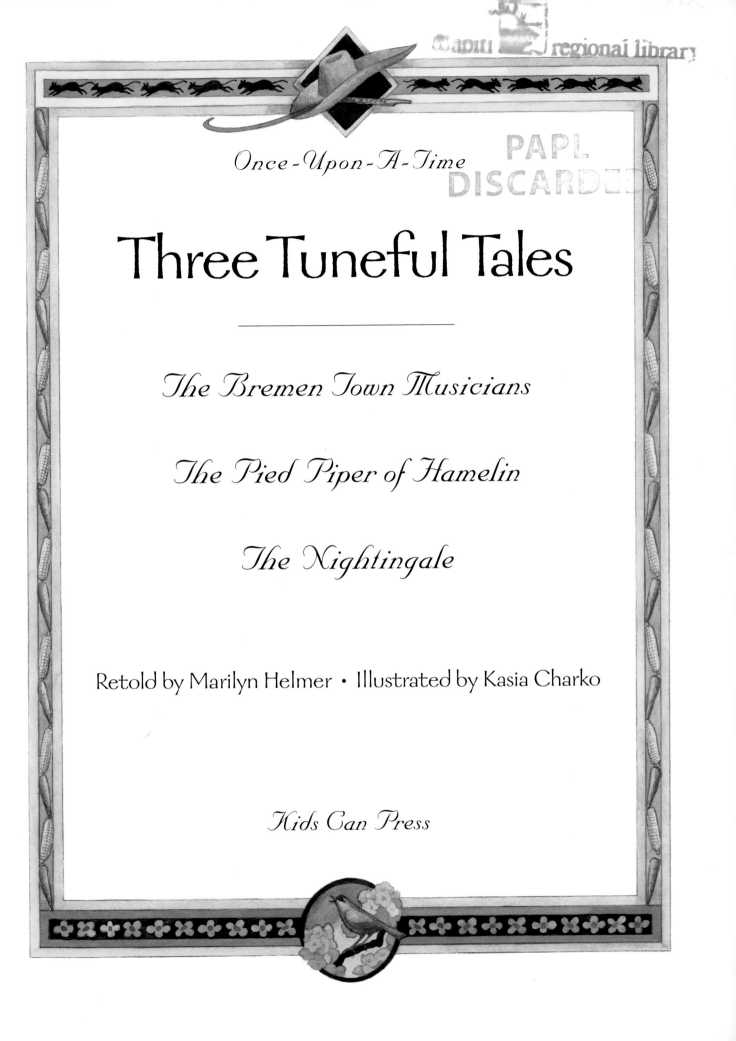

Once-Upon-A-Time

Three Tuneful Tales

The Bremen Town Musicians

The Pied Piper of Hamelin

The Nightingale

Retold by Marilyn Helmer • Illustrated by Kasia Charko

Kids Can Press

For Ruth Smith, J. Barbara Rose and teachers everywhere whose words and wisdom are music to the soul. — M. H.

To Karen. — K. C.

Text © 2003 Marilyn Helmer
Illustrations © 2003 Kasia Charko

Kids Can Press acknowledges the financial support of the Ontario Arts Council, the Canada Council for the Arts and the Government of Canada, through the BPIDP, for our publishing activity.

Published in Canada by
Kids Can Press Ltd.
29 Birch Avenue
Toronto, ON M4V 1E2

Published in the U.S. by
Kids Can Press Ltd.
2250 Military Road
Tonawanda, NY 14150

www.kidscanpress.com

The artwork in this book was rendered in watercolor.
Text is set in Berkeley.

Series Editor: Debbie Rogosin
Editor: David MacDonald
Design: Marie Bartholomew
Printed in Hong Kong, China, by Wing King Tong Company Limited

This book is smyth sewn casebound.

CM 03 0 9 8 7 6 5 4 3 2 1

National Library of Canada Cataloguing in Publication Data

Helmer, Marilyn
    Three tuneful tales / retold by Marilyn Helmer ; illustrated by Kasia Charko.

(Once-upon-a-time)
Complete contents: The Pied Piper of Hamelin — The Bremen town musicians — The nightingale.

ISBN 1-55074-941-2

1. Fairy tales. I. Charko, Kasia, 1949– II. Title. III. Series: Helmer, Marilyn. Once-upon-a-time.

PS8565.E4594T475 2003   j398.2   C2002-902206-1PZ8

Kids Can Press is a *lorus*™ Entertainment company

Contents

The Bremen Town Musicians

There was once a faithful Donkey who had served his master long and well. One day the Donkey overheard his master making plans to get rid of him. "The old beast must go, for he no longer earns his keep," the master said to his wife. "All he does now is bray and eat."

"Let's sell him to the tanner," suggested the wife. "Surely his hide must be worth a few pennies."

But the Donkey wasn't about to be made into a pair of leather boots! He had a plan of his own. "My bray is as lovely as any singing voice," he said to himself. "I will run away to Bremen and earn my living as a town musician." With that, the Donkey trotted off to seek his fortune.

He had not gone far when he met an old Dog sitting by the side of the road, howling. "What a fine voice you have!" exclaimed the Donkey.

"Not fine enough to please my master," said the Dog. "He has turned me out of the house because I'm too old to hunt."

"Come with me," suggested the Donkey. "I'm on my way to Bremen to become a town musician. Certainly two voices will be better than one."

"How kind of you to invite me," said the Dog, and he and the Donkey set off together.

Down the road they met a Cat, sitting on a fence, yowling. "What a splendid voice you have!" exclaimed the Donkey.

"Not splendid enough to please my mistress," said the Cat. "She will no longer keep me because I'm too slow to catch mice."

"Would you like to come with us?" asked the Dog. "We're going to Bremen to become town musicians. I'm sure that three voices will be better than two."

"I'd be delighted," said the Cat, and so the three animals walked along together.

Further on they met a Rooster, perched on a rooftop, crowing. "What a magnificent voice you have!" exclaimed the Donkey.

"Not magnificent enough to please the farmer," said the Rooster. "He plans to toss me into the stew pot because I slept past sunrise this morning and didn't wake him up."

"You must come along with us," said the Cat. "We're off to Bremen to become town musicians. Four voices will be even better than three."

"That's a fine idea," said the Rooster. So, with the Donkey in the lead, the four animals went on their way.

As they walked along the road to Bremen, the Donkey began to bray in time to the *clip-clop* of his feet. Soon the others joined in, howling, yowling and crowing at the top of their lungs. The four friends were having such a good time, they didn't notice that the other travelers were standing aside with their hands over their ears.

When darkness fell, the animals found themselves at the edge of a forest. By then they were tired and hungry, and needed a comfortable place to spend the night.

"I'll have a look around," said the Rooster. He flew up into a tall tree. "Good news!" he called down to the others. "I see a light in the distance."

"Hurrah!" cheered the Donkey. "Let's go and have a closer look."

The four friends made their way through the forest until they came to a house. When they peeked in the window, their eyes almost popped out of their heads! In the middle of the room was a table covered with the most wonderful assortment of good things to eat. Around the table, laughing and feasting, sat a band of rowdy robbers.

"Oh, how I'd like some of that delicious roast beef," said the Dog, pressing his nose against the window.

"The clotted cream looks so tasty," sighed the Cat. "But I don't suppose they'd share."

"A few ears of that corn would fill my stomach," added the Rooster. "If only we could get inside!"

"There must be some way to get rid of those robbers," declared the Donkey. The four animals talked it over and soon came up with a plan.

"Now let's get ready for our grand debut!" said the Donkey. He put his forelegs up on the windowsill. The Dog climbed on the Donkey's back. The Cat jumped onto the Dog's shoulders. And the Rooster perched on the Cat's head.

All at once the Donkey brayed and the Cat yowled, the Rooster crowed and the Dog howled. They crashed through the window, singing at the top of their lungs and scattering glass in all directions.

The robbers were so terrified that they raced out the door, leaving their delicious feast behind. Pushing one another aside, they fled into the forest and hid among the trees.

"We got rid of them in a hurry," said the Donkey.

"Some people just don't appreciate fine music," said the Dog.

"We've certainly earned our supper," said the Cat.

"Let's eat!" crowed the Rooster.

The four musicians helped themselves to the feast. After they had eaten their fill, each one found a comfortable spot to spend the night. The Donkey put out the lights and they all settled down to sleep.

Meanwhile, from their hiding places, the robbers had been watching the house. When they saw the lights go out, the boldest robber crept back to see what on earth was going on.

He slipped quietly through the door. It was so dark inside that the robber could scarcely see his hand in front of his face. As he made his way to the kitchen to find a candle, he spotted two glowing yellow dots by the fireplace. Those dots were the Cat's eyes, for she was still wide awake. But the robber mistook them for live coals and rushed over to light a match.

The robber didn't see the Donkey lying in front of him. He tripped, flew head over heels and landed on the floor with a thud.

The noise woke the other animals, and all four of them set upon the robber at once. The Donkey kicked at him, bucking and braying. The Cat jumped on him, scratching and yowling. The Rooster flew at him, pecking and crowing. And the Dog lunged at him, biting and howling. Frightened out of his wits, the robber dashed out the door as fast as his legs could carry him.

He ran back to his comrades and gasped, "There's a long-eared monster who kicks and brays ... a wicked witch who scratches and yowls ... a creature with claws who jabs and crows ... and a horrible hound who bites and howls. I barely escaped with my life!"

The robbers fled in terror, and I do believe they are running still. As for the four musicians, they decided to stay in the little house in the forest, for they were very happy there. Every night they sing for their supper. And, since they only sing to each other, nobody minds at all.

The Pied Piper of Hamelin

Long ago, on the banks of the Weser River, stood the busy town of Hamelin, just as it stands today. A finer town you've never seen, except for one thing. Rats! Hamelin was overrun by rats. Big rats, fat rats, mean rats, bold rats — rats were everywhere. They chased the dogs, bit the cats and frightened the children at play. All day long and through the night, they skittered and scattered into pantries and kitchens, chewing the cheeses, slurping the soup and devouring anything else they could find. And what a racket those rats made! They squeaked and squealed until the townsfolk had to stuff cotton in their ears, just to have a little peace and quiet.

Finally the people of Hamelin could stand it no longer. In a huge angry mob, they descended on the Town Hall to confront the Mayor. "Do whatever you have to, but get rid of the rats," the townsfolk demanded. "Every last one!"

As the angry mob surrounded him, the Mayor shook in his boots. He quickly turned to his Chief Councillor and ordered, "Get rid of the rats!"

The Chief Councillor turned to the next councillor. "Get rid of the rats," he said.

One by one, the councillors passed the order down the line. "Get rid of the rats! Get rid of the rats!"

Finally the last councillor scratched his head and asked, "But how?"

Silence fell over the Town Hall. No one, not the Mayor himself or a single councillor, could think of a way to rid Hamelin of the pesky rats.

Suddenly three sharp raps echoed through the Town Hall. The door flew open and in walked the most peculiar-looking stranger the people had ever seen. He was tall and thin as a willow stick, and wore a patchwork suit of bright red and yellow. His pointy-toed shoes looked as if they were made for dancing. From his neck hung a carved wooden pipe. "Your Honor," he said, removing his hat and bowing deeply, "I have come to rid Hamelin of the rats."

The Mayor eyed the stranger suspiciously. "Who are you?" he demanded. "And how will you get rid of the rats?"

"I am called the Pied Piper," the stranger replied with an odd little smile. "When I play my magic pipe, the rats will follow me wherever I go. No living creature can resist the charm of my music."

"How much will we have to pay you?" asked the Chief Councillor.

"One thousand guilders," replied the Pied Piper.

"Agreed," said the Mayor immediately. "Just get rid of the rats!"

The Pied Piper stepped out into the bright noonday sun. He put the pipe to his lips and blew a haunting melody into the air. And then, from holes and hiding places, from cellars and attics, from shops and storerooms, the rats came. Big rats, fat rats, mean rats, bold rats — not a single one could resist the strange sweet music.

As the Pied Piper made his way from street to street, the rats gathered behind him like a miniature army. Squeaking and squealing, dancing and reeling, they followed the music as if bewitched.

On and on the Pied Piper led them, until he came to the edge of the Weser River. Without missing a note, he waded right in. As the townsfolk watched in disbelief, the rats plunged in after him. The Pied Piper played on until every last rat was swallowed up by the churning water.

The townsfolk cheered and the councillors applauded. The Mayor breathed a sigh of relief. All through the town, bells rang out and everyone danced in the streets. But in the midst of the celebrations, the Pied Piper appeared again. "My work is done, Your Honor," he said to the Mayor. "I will take my thousand guilders, if you please."

The Mayor frowned. The councillors scowled. The townsfolk glared and shook their heads. Now that the rats were gone, the people of Hamelin could think of much better ways to spend a thousand guilders than to give it to this stranger.

The Mayor cleared his throat and drew himself up to full height. "Come now, my good fellow," he said. "All you did was play your pipe. With our own eyes we saw the rats drown themselves in the Weser River. Dead rats are not worth a thousand guilders," he added with a smirk. "We will pay you fifty guilders."

All eyes turned to the Pied Piper. His face grew dark with anger and his odd little smile appeared again. These were the words he spoke:

Cheat me and you'll rue the day
The Pied Piper came your way!

"Fifty guilders or nothing at all," the Mayor said sharply. The councillors nodded in agreement.

"Your work is done!" shouted the townsfolk. "Take the money and go!"

Without a word, the Pied Piper lifted the pipe to his lips and, once again, blew a haunting melody into the air. This time, clapping and clattering, skipping and chattering, the children came. The Pied Piper made his way from street to street, gathering the children just as he had gathered the rats. Not a single child could resist the strange sweet music. With cheeks aglow and eyes sparkling, they ran after the Pied Piper. And no one, not mothers or fathers, not aunts or uncles, not even the Mayor or his councillors, could stop them.

On and on the Pied Piper led the children, across the town and far away, right to Koppelberg Hill. As they drew near — lo and behold — a door opened in the side of the hill. Beyond was a beautiful forest where birds sang and deer played among the trees.

The children followed the Pied Piper through the door and into the forest. Then the door swung shut behind them. Neither the Piper nor the children were ever seen again.

So that their beloved children would never be forgotten, the people of Hamelin had a memorial carved on the side of Koppelberg Hill. At the base of the memorial, these words were inscribed:

> *We would not pay the Piper's cost;*
> *Our precious children now are lost.*
> *To all we offer this advice:*
> *'Tis best to pay the Piper's price.*

The Nightingale

Many years ago in China, there lived a rich and powerful Emperor. In all the world, there was not a palace as magnificent as his. It was built of the finest porcelain, with crystal floors and doors of solid gold. Ivory-framed windows looked out over a splendid garden surrounded by terraces and pools filled with exotic fish.

Only the rarest and loveliest flowers grew in the Emperor's garden. To the most exquisite of these, tiny silver bells were attached. With the slightest breeze, the bells tinkled like dainty chimes, drawing attention to the delicate blooms. Beyond the garden lay the Emperor's great forest, which stretched to the edge of the sea.

In the forest lived a Nightingale with a voice so sweet that all who heard it stopped to listen. Chattering squirrels fell silent and fishermen paused as they cast their nets. Even the fish in the sea swam closer to the surface whenever the Nightingale sang.

Travelers came from across the land to admire the splendor of the Emperor's palace and the beauty of his gardens. But when they heard the Nightingale's song, they were amazed. "This bird is the greatest treasure of all!" they declared.

Stories of the Emperor's magnificent estate spread far and wide. Scholars wrote books describing the riches it held. One day the Emperor himself read one of these books. He was overcome with pride to see his possessions so highly praised. But when he came to the words *The greatest wonder of all is the Nightingale*, he was astonished.

"How can this be?" he gasped. "There is such a remarkable bird among my possessions, yet I have never heard it sing! Why has no one told me of this treasure?" He summoned his Chief Advisor. "Find this Nightingale and bring it to me at once," ordered the Emperor.

"Right away, my Lord," said the Chief Advisor, and he hurried off to do the Emperor's bidding.

After questioning many people in the palace, he found a kitchen maid who had actually heard the Nightingale. "I listen to its song each evening when I walk through the forest," she said. "The music is so pure and sweet, it brings joy to my heart."

"Show me this Nightingale and you shall have the job of head kitchen maid," said the Chief Advisor.

"Follow me, Sir," said the kitchen maid, and she led him to a tree at the edge of the forest.

When the Chief Advisor saw the little brown bird, he was not impressed. "Could so plain a creature sing so beautifully?" he wondered. But when the Nightingale burst into song, the Chief Advisor was enchanted. "Indeed, its voice sounds like the ringing of crystal bells," he murmured.

Bowing before the little bird, the Chief Advisor said, "Wondrous Nightingale, the Emperor wishes you to sing at his palace."

"I would rather sing here in the forest," said the Nightingale, "but I will do as the Emperor requests."

That evening, the entire court gathered to hear the Nightingale sing. Even the kitchen maid was allowed to attend. Excited whispers filled the Great Hall. Finally the Emperor arrived and took his place on the throne. Immediately after, the Chief Advisor entered with the little bird on his shoulder. As he placed the Nightingale on a gilded perch, an expectant hush fell over the room. The Emperor nodded his head, and the Nightingale began to sing. A song of such rare beauty poured from the little bird's throat that people listened spellbound.

The song moved the Emperor to tears. "I will give you my golden slipper to wear around your neck," he declared.

The Nightingale thanked the Emperor for his generous offer. "But I cannot accept your slipper," he said. "It is an honor to sing for you, and your tears are the greatest reward of all."

From that day on, the Nightingale lived at the palace. The Emperor presented him with a cage of solid gold and appointed twelve servants to look after him. Every day the little bird was allowed to leave the cage for a few minutes, but the servants made sure that he could not escape. At the Emperor's order, they tied twelve silk ribbons to the Nightingale's legs. Each servant held one of the ribbons so the Nightingale could no longer fly free.

Then one day a package arrived for the Emperor. Inside was a most remarkable gift from the emperor of Japan. It was a mechanical nightingale, fashioned by a clever clockmaker to look like the real one. But this nightingale was made of the finest gold and studded with diamonds, rubies and sapphires. Around its neck was a ribbon with the words *The Nightingale of Japan is but a poor shadow beside the Nightingale of China*. At the turn of a key, sweet music poured from the bird's bejeweled throat while its tail flicked up and down.

The Emperor clapped his hands in delight. "Now the two nightingales must sing together," he said, placing the birds side by side. But alas, although each sang beautifully, they did not sing in harmony. The real Nightingale sang different notes every time, while the mechanical one sang the same song over and over.

"We certainly cannot blame the new bird," said the Music Master disdainfully. "Its timing and notes follow the rules of music perfectly."

From that day on, the Emperor and his court listened only to the song of the mechanical nightingale. It could sing for hours without tiring, and the bejeweled bird was far more beautiful to look at than the real Nightingale.

Then a day came when the Emperor wished to hear the real Nightingale again. But the little brown bird was nowhere to be found. While everyone's attention was on the mechanical bird, the real one had flown back to his forest home. The Emperor was furious. "Is this the way he repays the honor of living in luxury at my palace?" he fumed. "I hereby banish him from my empire!" After that, the real Nightingale was never mentioned again. In time his beautiful song was all but forgotten.

One night, as the Emperor lay in bed listening to the mechanical nightingale, a terrible thing happened. With a dreadful grinding and clanking, it stopped singing. The Emperor summoned the Music Master and ordered him to repair the bird at once. With much difficulty, the Music Master was able to restore the bird's song. "I have managed to fix the gears, but they are almost worn out," he told the Emperor. "It will be impossible to replace them without damaging the sound. From now on, the mechanical bird must sing only once a year."

Five years passed and then a great sorrow fell over the land. The Emperor was very ill, so ill that a new Emperor was chosen to become his successor. One day a rumor went through the palace that the old Emperor had died. Believing the rumor to be true, the courtiers quickly hurried off to pledge their loyalty to the new Emperor.

But the old Emperor had not yet drawn his last breath. Alone in his bedchamber, he longed to hear the nightingale's song. With a trembling hand he reached out to the mechanical bird. Try as he might, he was too weak to wind it up. "Sing for me once more," pleaded the Emperor, but to no avail. Tears came to his eyes as he remembered the real Nightingale, whose song was just as beautiful, yet different every time.

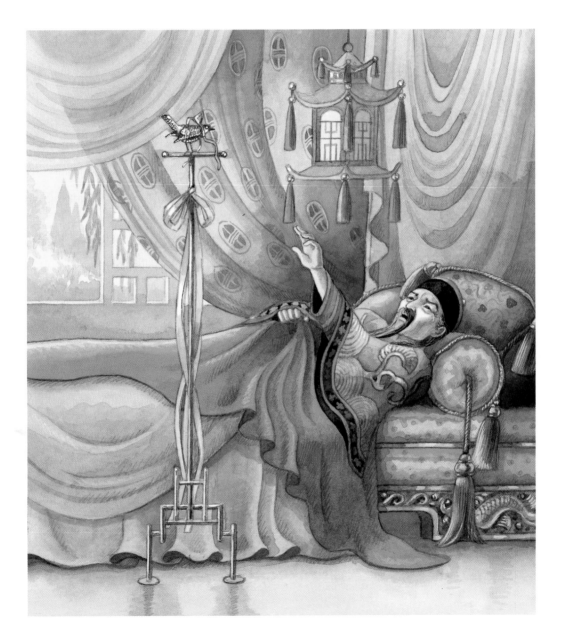

At that moment there was a gentle flutter of wings, and the little brown bird appeared on the windowsill. "Precious Nightingale!" exclaimed the Emperor. "You have come back to me, even after I so thoughtlessly banished you from my empire."

"I will sing for you, gracious Emperor," said the Nightingale. As the pure clear notes poured from the bird's throat, life surged back into the Emperor's body. A smile came to his lips. "You must come and live with me in the palace forever," he said.

"Let me live free and I will return every evening," said the Nightingale. "I will sing for you and bring all the news of the countryside so that you can rule wisely and well. But you must promise not to tell a soul that a little bird comes to visit and offers his advice."

"I give you my word," said the Emperor. The Nightingale flew away and the Emperor fell into a deep restful sleep.

The next morning, the Chief Advisor led a sad procession of courtiers to the Emperor's bedchamber. They had come to pay their last respects, for they believed that the Emperor was dead.

As the courtiers entered the bedchamber, the sun shone through the window and the Emperor opened his eyes. Imagine how astonished they were when he sat up and greeted them with a joyful "Good morning!"

The Emperor lived for many more years, and he became known throughout the land as the wisest of rulers. Every evening he was cheered by the Nightingale's song, and no one ever found out that the little brown bird was the Emperor's secret advisor.